UNCL

HOO I

An Easy Peasy Person
from Easy Peasy Island
in the middle of the Terrific Ocean

Pan

Uncle Hoot is the wise old owl of Easy Peasy Island.
At least, he thinks he is.
But he isn't really.
In fact, he is very, very, very silly.
As you'll find out.
He lives in Featherbed Cottage, up a tree, in the middle of Whistling Wood, next door to his friend Bill Buzz.

All the Easy Peasy people used to come and see Uncle Hoot when they wanted to know something. And Uncle Hoot would pretend to know the answer.
Even though he didn't!

You can usually find Uncle Hoot
on the lowest branch of the highest
tree in Whistling Wood.
And that is where Charlie Oink,
the Easy Peasy pig, found him.

"Why do flowers grow upwards?" asked Charlie Oink.

Uncle Hoot fluffed out his feathers and said in a very important voice: "Because, if flowers didn't grow upwards, they would grow downwards, and we would have to stand on our heads to see them properly."

"Oh," said Charlie Oink.

Horace Honk, the Easy Peasy Island seal, came along.
"Why does rain fall from the sky?" he asked.
Uncle Hoot fluffed out his feathers and hooted in an even more important voice:
"Because if rain didn't fall down, then it would fall up and people's umbrellas wouldn't work."
"Oh," said Horace.

Trevor Trunk, the Easy Peasy
Island elephant, came along.
He raised his trunk in the air.
"Yes?" asked Uncle Hoot.
Trevor looked around him in a
blank sort of way.
"I've forgotten," admitted Trevor.
You remember, Trevor Trunk has
a dreadful memory.
Or perhaps you've forgotten!

Harry Hoof, the Easy Peasy Island horse, was wondering something. "Why don't trees talk?" he asked. Uncle Hoot fluffed out his feathers and said in a most extraordinarily important voice:
"Because if trees could talk this wood would be a very noisy place to live!"
"Oh," said Harry.

"RUBBISH!" said a very deep, echoing voice.
Uncle Hoot almost fell off the lowest branch of the tallest tree in Whistling Wood.

"Who said that?" asked Uncle Hoot.
"I DID!" replied the deep, echoing
voice.
"Who's 'I'?" asked Uncle Hoot again.
"Me!" said the deep, echoing voice
again. "And you're standing on me!"
It was the tree talking!

"But trees don't talk!" spluttered Uncle Hoot.

"So you said," said the tree. "You were wrong, weren't you?"

"Wrong?" hooted Uncle Hoot. "Me? But I'm the wise old owl of Easy Peasy Island!"

"Most certainly old," said the tree. "But not particularly wise."

Poor Uncle Hoot said, in a rather unimportant voice, "Oh."
And he flew off into the wood feeling a lot less wise than he had when he woke up that morning.

Now what you don't know, what Uncle Hoot didn't know, and what none of the other Easy Peasy people knew, was that Sam Squeak had been sitting inside the hollow trunk of the tallest tree in Whistling Wood all morning. Listening.

And I'm sure that you can guess whose voice Uncle Hoot had really heard booming from inside the tree.
Yes, that's right.
Sam Squeak's!
Sam had been playing tricks on Uncle Hoot.
Sam started to chuckle.
The chuckle turned into a giggle.
The giggle turned into a laugh that boomed and echoed through the whole of Whistling Wood.
HO! HO! HO!

Still laughing, Sam Squeak popped his head through a hole in the side of the tree and winked at Harry Hoof, Trevor Trunk, Horace Honk and Charlie Oink.
As soon as they saw Sam Squeak, they knew what he had done.
They smiled and they grinned and they chuckled and they laughed.
And laughed and laughed and laughed.

"In future," laughed Sam, "you had better ask me . . . Tee! Hee! Hee! . . . anything you want to know. Ho! Ho! Ho!"

Charlie Oink looked at him.

"Why is the sky blue?" he asked.

Sam thought.
"I've no idea," he said, and giggled.
Tee! Hee! Hee!